ABUELITA ROSA

PARA MI ABUELITA,
QUE ME ESTÁ CUIDANDO
DESDE EL CIELO ♥

Lil' LIBROS

www.LilLibros.com

Published in the United States by Lil' Libros

ISBN: 978-1-948066-21-1

Library of Congress Control Number: 2021944813

Printed in China

First Edition, 2022

27 26 25 24 23 22   5 4 3 2 1

MiLo + NiKo

ART + STORY BY
D GUZMÁN

Milo was stuck in her abuelita's plant shop for the day.

Milo se sentía encerrada todo el día en la tienda de plantas de su abuelita.

"When are you going to play with me?" a bored Milo asked.
"Milo, I'm busy right now, but I'm sure if you look around
you can find many treasures in places you don't expect."

—¿Cuándo vas a jugar conmigo? —preguntó Milo muy aburrida.
—Milo, estoy ocupada en este momento, pero estoy segura
de que si miras a tu alrededor puedes encontrar
muchos tesoros en lugares que no esperas.—

ABUELITA

Curious, Milo wandered off...

Curiosa, Milo se fue a explorar...

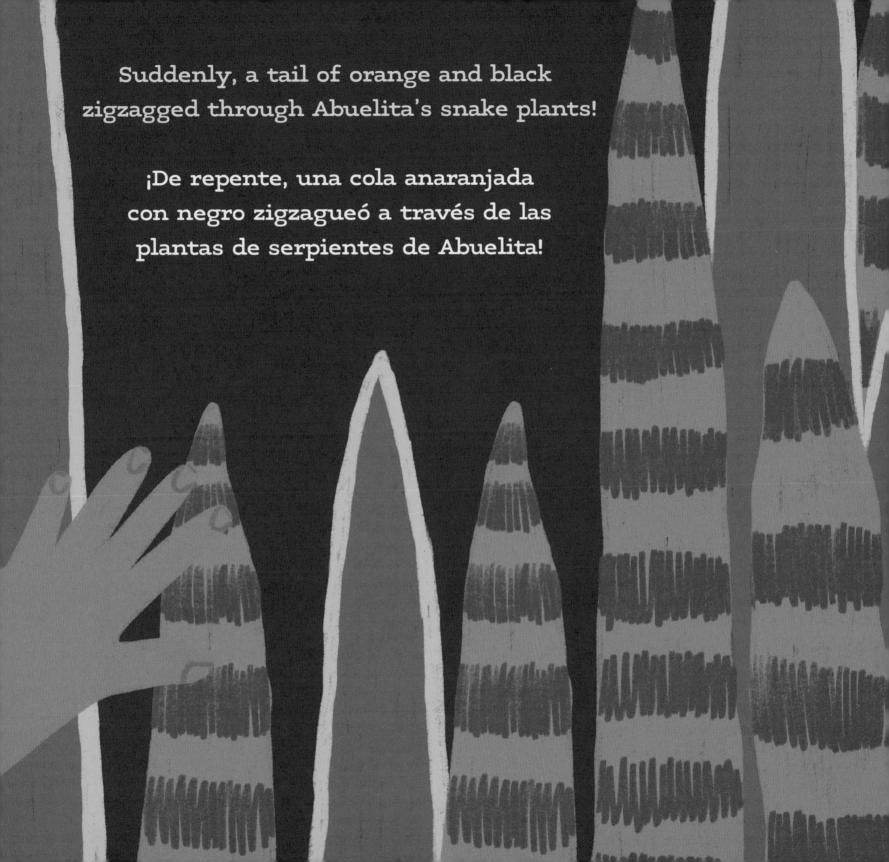

Suddenly, a tail of orange and black zigzagged through Abuelita's snake plants!

¡De repente, una cola anaranjada con negro zigzagueó a través de las plantas de serpientes de Abuelita!

Milo found a friend
"I'm going to name you..."

Milo encontró un amigo.
—Te voy a nombrar...

Niko, you and I are going to go
on an adventure together...
in the deep... dark... JUNGLE."

—Niko, tú y yo vamos a emprender
una aventura juntos... en lo profundo...
en lo oscuro... de la SELVA.—

And off they went.

Y se fueron juntos.

Ellos buscaron...

They explored...

Exploraron...

They sailed...

Navegaron...

Milo and Niko were having
so much fun they didn't realize
Abuelita was already closing the shop.

Milo y Niko se estaban divirtiendo tanto
que no se dieron cuenta de que
Abuelita ya estaba cerrando la tienda.

"Milo, it's time to go home," said Abuelita.
"Look at my treasure!" exclaimed Milo.
"His name is Niko, can we take him home?"
"Hmmm, I have an idea," answered Abuelita.

—Milo, es hora de irse a casa —dijo Abuelita.
—¡Mira mi tesoro! —exclamó Milo.
—Su nombre es Niko, ¿podemos llevarlo a casa?—
—Hmmm, tengo una idea —respondió Abuelita.

Abuelita grabbed
an apron.

Abuelita tomó
un delantal.

A large pot.

Una maceta grande.

A small pot.

Una maceta pequeña.

And a bag of soil.

Y una bolsa de tierra.

"How about Niko stays here to
protect the plants?" Abuelita suggested.
She placed the soil and apron inside the largest pot,
then filled the smallest pot with water.
Niko stretched out, glad to be in his new bed.

—¿Qué tal si Niko se queda aquí
para proteger las plantas? —sugirió Abuelita.
Colocó la tierra y el delantal dentro de la maceta
más grande, luego llenó la maceta más pequeña con agua.
Niko se estiró, contento de estar en su nueva cama.

Seeing that Niko was content,
Abuelita grabbed the keys out
of her purse and locked up
her beloved shop.

Al ver que Niko estaba contento,
Abuelita tomó las llaves de su bolsa
y cerró su amada tienda.

Milo was filled with excitement as she looked back and waved goodbye. Who knows what treasures tomorrow would bring with her new best friend Niko.

Milo se llenó de emoción cuando miró hacia atrás
y se despidió. Quién sabe qué tesoros traerá mañana
con su nuevo mejor amigo Niko.

ABUELITA ROSA

Milo + Niko was inspired by my own Abuelita Rosa who passed away in October 2019. Although she didn't have her own shop, her love of plants and her home in Mexico was the inspiration for this book.

Abuelita Rosa united the Guzmán family with her kind heart. She was the sweetest grandmother and always made sure everyone was well taken care of before herself. My love for her is reflected back in this book.

My Abuelita will truly be missed and loved forever.

I hope this story inspires you to create your own journey at your Abuelita's home and remember to hold her hand extra tight.

– D Guzmán

D Guzmán is a Latine illustrator for picture books and freelance work. She lives in Minneapolis, MN with her partner, two cats, dog, many fish, and her own jungle of houseplants. D loves to take road trips and travel with her partner to find inspiration.

When she's not illustrating children's books, she runs an at-home print shop and creates and sells her own illustration prints online. D has worked with Target and Pollen Midwest. She has exhibited her work with Family Tree Clinic and Light Grey Art Lab. Her website is: Dtheartista.com.